A THE TOP COP SERIES

VICTIM
THE BOOK
REASON BEHIND THE CRIME

A BOOK BY SSM types

EDITED BY
M.A.N

PRINTED BY

notionpress.com

First Edition.
First Published - July'18

ISBN 978-93-5311-601-9

This is a work of fiction.
Name(s) or character(s), business(es) or place(s), event(s) or incident(s), restaurant(s) or café(s) are either the products of the author's imagination or used in a fictitious manner. Any resemblance to anyone or anything, living or dead, existing or non-existing, running or closed, present or past, is purely coincidental.

Written by
SSMtypes (pen-name of Syed Sufwan Mohiuddin)
Edited by
M.A.N (pen-name of Mohd Safwan Hussain)
Cover and Victim the Book, The Top Cop Series, **SSM**types, M.A.N logo designed by
Ineative (@beineative)
Printed by
Notion Press Media Pvt. Ltd.

"*Where were you?*" I asked a tall man, standing in front of me; with grey hair and fair skin; looking at his dead wife, lying on the floor in the kitchen, in front of us, who was shot dead. The kitchen was neat and clean, no sign of scuffle.

"*I was in the office*" he replied, with his eyes still on his wife. I kept my right hand on his left shoulder which meant 'Be strong mate'. In reply, he turned his face to me and nodded which meant 'Yes I will; thanks for your concern'.

"*So you usually come home by this time?*" I asked him.

Now totally turning himself to me, "*No I usually come by 8, but today, we planned to have dinner outside... so... but...*" He replied as tears rolled down his cheeks.

Do people go for dinner in the evening at 4? Or is he just lying? May be he might've murdered his wife and pretending to be innocent. No doubt he would be our prime suspect. Standing in a duplex furnished house with some minimum essentials. He called us at 4:15pm and informed about his wife and we were here by 4:37pm.

"*Sir... no murder weapon*" said Addy; Addison Bishop – a Speedy Investigation Department Officer of Indust City Crime Branch, my junior; after searching the whole house. We call it SID of ICCB in short. I went near to the dead body of Mrs. Ana Thomson wife-of Mr. Jose Thomson.

"*Tell me*" I enquired Sam; Samuel Crompton - also Speedy Investigation Department Officer from ICCB, my junior. I've one more officer in my team, Joseph Noakes, who's on leave for a couple of days to celebrate the birth of his first infant. All of them reliable and audacious officers, I have got the best as a team.

"*She was shot with a 9x19mm Parabellum round from a proximity and no sign of struggle on her body*" Sam informed.

I went to Jose who was sitting on sofa, deeply thinking or maybe just pretending to be, "*Jose, the door would be usually locked from inside... right?*" I questioned him.

He turned his face to me still sitting on sofa and responded "*Yes, it's usually locked from inside.*"

And continued after a quick pause "*But today when I returned, the door was already open. I entered hesitantly and shouted for her... but in vain... searching for her, I entered kitchen and found her...*" he stopped as he started crying again.

"*Do you doubt anyone?*" I asked him to which he replied "*No, none.*"

That means, someone who was close to her, who she had no fear of, has shot her to dead. We then gathered all the necessary evidence(s) including her mobile phone and fingerprints from all over the house.

"*We'll call you upon need, Mr. Jose. Be in touch and don't leave the city, until the case is solved*" I said to Jose.

"*Okay Officer*" he replied and accompanied us to our jeep. "*I want my wife's murderer to be caught soon... that bastard took my love away from me... she was the only one I was living for*" said he, speaking for the longest time since we met.

"*Of course*" I consoled him as we left his place.

***

We drove back to our office; a big glass building with not so high security – who would rob a place where the SID of ICCB is.

"*Find out about Jose, all detailed report on him from the first thing he does in the morning to the last thing he does before sleeping*" I ordered Addy as we walked in to our cabin.

"*If possible let me know what he dreams too*" I joked, smiling. He and Sam, both laughed. Joking around during work without affecting it to the work is necessary. I read it somewhere that 'A sense of humor is part of the art of leadership, of getting along with people, of getting things done.'

"*Why are you laughing? ... Go to forensic lab along with the fingerprints and other evidences*" I said to Sam with an angry face that made him little scared but then I laughed and Addy too joined me.

"*Okay get back to work guys*" I said as they went on to execute the tasks. I believe there's always a Reason behind every Crime. And that's why I'm focusing on the possible reasons anyone would've, to murder Ana. In most of the cases, an extra marital affair, property, money, anything of that sort.

***

"*Sir the fingerprints are only of Ana's & Jose's in the house*" Sam said as he walked into my cabin after a while.

And continued "*Ana's phone also has nothing suspicious... just some calls to her brother, friends and constantly to Jose... and a few casual pictures.*"

"*Hmm... so nothing for us*" I replied him and continued after a second pause "*Anyhow Jose is still my prime suspect.*"

Few minutes of silence in the room ended as I spoke "*Sam till Addy checks up on Jose, you do a check on Ana... track down every possible thing about her... her family, in-laws, friends, anyone who she messed up with and anyone who had a benefit after her death*" I said him to which he nodded in reply and left.

***

As I was busy with my thoughts. Addison and Samuel were just working, I guess. But what's taking them so long? Or they went home? To give their wives the grocery? They are taking longer than I expected. I am out of thoughts. And as I just thought about them, both Addy and Sam came in.

"*Sir*" they both called me together.

"*Addy you first*" I said.

"*Sir, Jose is clean, no extra marital affair, phone call history doesn't suggest any suspicion, no fights, no controversies*" said Addy. I'm surprised to hear that because it makes my prime suspect clean and innocent.

"*And what've you got?*" I asked Sam.

"*Sir, even she had no extra martial affair or any such relation in past*" he answered.

"*Strange*" I replied and he continued "*One thing, her father owned a property, an old house, right in middle of a commercial area on Corporate Road.*"

"*That's quite an expensive one, at a prime location*" I said nodding my head.

"*Yes*" they both replied "*Where is her dad now?*" I asked to which Sam replied "*A few months ago, her parents passed away in a car accident... She has got a brother living with his own family in a JS Colony in Tietan.*"

"*So according to the law that prime property now belongs to Ana and her brother*" I said and questioned Sam "*Her father... did he make any will?*"

To which he replied "*Nope*" and again continued "*And whereas of friends she just has a few closed one's... and again nothing suspicious.*"

"*So the only one who gets benefitted with her death is her brother*" I replied and continued after a minute pause "*And that property is the reason*" and went into deep thinking.

"*Hey get me CCTV footages of all nearby installed CCTV cameras near their residence*" I ordered Addy and before Addy could leave I continued "*And what about their neighbors?*"

To which Addy replied "*Sir their neighbor is family of three… the couple was on work and their daughter was in the college*" and he left.

"*Sam contact their neighbors and also Ana's brother*" I ordered Sam and he too left, leaving me alone in the room again.

***

"*Sir neighbors said they've no idea about Jose and Ana, they just wish each other upon encounter*" Sam said as he came back after a few minutes and continued "*Brenden is in shock... even he has no doubt on anyone.*"

***

Soon Addy too came in along with CCTV Camera footages and handed it over Sam.

"*Fortunately, there's a CCTV camera in front of their residence focusing the entrance*" Addy said as Sam played the footage.

We started watching. Let's see what this CCTV Camera footage has to say.

No one entering during the assumed murdered time i.e. 3pm to 4pm. Jose leaving the house in the morning at 8:30am. Just a few buses stopping right in front of their house, which interrupts our view. Jose returning back at 4:20pm. No one in between. None.

This seems to be a well-planned murder, someone who knew, there's a CCTV Camera focusing their entrance, and also bus-stop at their entrance and also that every time a bus stops there it interrupts the camera's view and cover who is entering the house. And the murderer sharply used the bus stop and entered the house while the bus interrupts the CCTV camera's view. Even Ana opened the door and welcomed. So the murderer is definitely someone who is close to her and frequently visits. Which could be her brother, Brenden; he has a big prime reason too.

"*Hey get me today's Jose's and Brenden's phone location*" I ordered Sam and he left.

"*Sir, Jose's phone call location says he was in the office from morning 9:30am to 4:00pm*" said Sam as he came after nearly 20 minutes while I and Addy were still watching footages from all the CCTV camera's in the targeted location and surroundings.

"*What about Ana's brother?*" I asked to which Sam replied "*His location says he was there at Ana's house from morning 9:00am till 3:40pm in the evening.*"

"*We got our culprit*" I replied and quickly commanded "*Go, get him.*"

And till then I decided to call Jose and get his views on Brenden.

"*Hello, Mr. Jose?*" I said as soon as he received my call.

"*Hello, yeah, who's this?*" responded Jose.

"*Charles, SID Officer*" I answered.

"*Oh yes, did you catch the culprit?*" he asked me.

"*Well… not yet… but we'll… soon*" I replied and asked him "*What you've to say about Ana's brother?*"

"*Brenden? I didn't get you… What do you mean by that?*" he replied.

"*Actually… We suspect on him*" I said him.

"*What???... Do you really think so? But why would he do that?*" he replied shockingly.

"Didn't you know about your father-in-law's property" I asked him.

"Yeah... The One at Corporate Road?" he said.

"Yes" I replied him and before I could say him anything he continued *"He asked Ana to sell her share in the property at low price."*

"Hmm... Jose we just suspect him... We are not concluding" I stated, not mentioning about Brenden's Phone Location.

"Officer... Officer... I don't really want to know about it... I just want Ana's murderer to be punished" he said angrily and quickly continued *"No matter whoever it is"*

"Mr. Jose... I'll make sure about that... and would inform you" I said him. Followed by *"Bye"* from both the sides as we ended the call.

Standing right in front of me, in his late 30s, our Suspect probably the actual culprit too, Ana's Brother, Brenden Gleeson.

"*Me????*" he replied shockingly.

"*Why would I kill my own sister?*" he continued as I was keenly observing his face. His facial expression says he's not lying.

"*Your phone location says you was there at Ana's house since morning and during the assumed murder time*" I said.

"*My phone????*" he replied, more shocked now, and continued "*My phone was stolen yesterday night near the supermarket.*"

"*Really?*" I asked him; don't know why I felt like trusting him.

"*Let's go to that supermarket now*" I said.

***

"*This is that supermarket*" said Brenden pointing at a supermarket located at a walkable distance from his house in JS Colony, Tietan and he walked a few steps in the direction of his house and said "*And here my phone was stolen as I was using it and someone just snatched it and ran away.*" We went to the supermarket and asked the employee at the counter to call their manager.

"*Charles... Speedy Investigation Department*" I said the manager showing him my ID.

"*Ohh. I'm Oliver... how may I help you?*" he introduced himself.

"*Can we check the CCTV footage*" I said.

"*Of course*" he replied and took us to his cabin.

"*Time?*" he asked as he settled himself on the operator's chair.

Before I could reply him Brenden interrupted and said "*Yesterday night 9:30.*"

"*Hmm...*" replied Oliver seeing Brenden from top to bottom.

"*That's me*" said Brenden pointing out himself with at the counter, on the computer screen.

But in this footage his back was facing the camera. "*Show footage of same time from different angle*" said Sam to Oliver who nodded his head and started searching for the footage. Looks like he found the desired angle now he is fast forwarding the footage.

"*Hhmm... here he is*" said Oliver pointing at Brenden on the computer screen. Brenden was right he was there in the supermarket but that doesn't prove that his phone was stolen. We should look for CCTVs outside the supermarket.

"*Show us footage of CCTV outside*" said Addy and Sam continued "*And Start from the same time.*" Addy looked at Sam smiling and they both then looked at me and I nodded my head with a smile which meant Good Work. This is what is called a perfect team.

Oliver showed us the footage of CCTV outside the supermarket. We could now see Brenden leaving the mart while using his phone and walking in the direction of his house and slowly fading out of focus. I doubt he is lying; lying about his lost phone.

We could see a guy riding bike, coming to Brenden, snatched his phone and rode away. Brenden is right his phone was stolen.

"*Zoom-in to that bike*" Addy said as Oliver zoomed-in only to find that the bike has no number plate and the guy riding it was completely hiding his face.

"*Give a copy of the footage to Addison*" I said to Oliver to which he replied "*Okay officer.*"

***

"*Sir, the rider seemed like a professional; the way he was riding the bike off road*" said Addy as we sat into the Jeep.

"*Do you know anyone who can ride bike that perfectly?*" I question Brenden.

"*No*" he responded and started to think and continued "*No I know no one who can ride bike that perfectly.*" Our Second Prime Suspect, Jose doesn't even have a bike but he could also rent one.

"*Brenden, we'll drop you at your home*" I said him and continued "*But you can't leave the city until the case is solved and we would call you whenever needed.*"

"*Can I see my sister's dead body at least*" he asked and continued "*I lost my sister and you guys are just suspecting me*" he said, weeping. And continued again "*Why would I kill her?*"

"*It's just our job to see every aspect*" I said him as I placed my hand on his back. "*Don't you want the murderer of your sister to be caught?*" I asked him to which he replied "*Yes, I want that bastard to be caught and punished for his deeds.*"

"*Then please cooperate with us till we find the actual culprit*" I said him as we reached Brenden's house. His wife and children came running from inside worried about why her husband and their father was arrested. We dropped him and left his place.

It's nearly 9:30 pm now; five hours passed to Ana's murder. And also the time for us to go back home but the inner-me says we would solve this within an hour from now. Neither Addy nor Sam has mentioned about the time; but I'm sure they might have noticed. Just as I was busy with my thoughts we reached office.

***

"*Let's start from the beginning*" I said them and he started watching the CCTV footages again. While I recalled the whole case.

Ana was murdered between 3pm to 4pm in the Kitchen. The murderer was someone she knew and have no fear of losing her life because she was headshot to death from a proximity.

Jose called us to inform. He came early that day because he says they planned to have dinner out, today.

CCTV Camera right in front of their entrance shows none entered the house entire day or may be someone entered, exactly when the camera's view was interrupted by buses stopping there.

Jose was in the office that day says him and his phone location. Brenden's phone location says he was at Ana's house all day and during the assumed murder time. He has the reason to kill his sister, the prime property their father owned that would now belong to him and Jose.

But he says his phone was stolen a night before and he didn't even know about it before we shared with him. Supermarket's CCTV says he's right.

So Brenden is clean, remains is Jose, even he would get Ana's share but his phone location say's he was at the office.

All these thoughts running through my head ended when Sam interrupted "*Sir we know Jose phone was at office entire but that doesn't really prove that he was there too.*"

"*Ohh Shit, how come we miss that simple yet important point...? Well done, Sam*" I said and continued "*Call Addy and ask him to find it out.*" So Jose must have hired someone to snatch Brenden's phone, and kept his phone at the office till 4pm and Brenden's phone at his residence because he knew we would check phone locations and after knowing that we would think Brenden is a culprit.

We would've believed his planned theory too but Brenden was fortunate that robbery of his phone was recorded on supermarket's CCTV.

And that's why he was home early, I suspected him from the starting. All these thoughts ended with one instant thought of mine.

"*Hey find when the last bus stopped there before 4:30pm*" I said and he started looking for it.

"*Sir*" called Sam and I went to the laptop. Last bus stopped at 3:40pm. And last second at 3:20pm. May be that's the time she was murdered in between 3:20pm and 3:40pm in those 20 minutes. 20 minutes of time is well enough to kill someone you know.

"Sammm... How much time would it take for Jose to travel from his office to home" Sam went on to calculate and soon replied *"Sir 20minutes."*

"So Jose entered house at 4:20pm so he must have left office at 4:00pm. The last bus stopped at 3:40pm surprisingly exactly 20 minutes before 4:00pm and the last second bus again surprisingly exactly 20 minutes before 3:40pm.

So now if we assume Jose himself killed his wife then he must have left the office at 3:00pm came home and entered hiding himself behind from the CCTV using the bus that stops at 3:20pm which allows him to enter house without being caught on CCTV then murdered his wife and left the house again using the bus that stops at 3:40pm which again helped him not to get caught on CCTV.

So he comes, murders and escapes leaving no proof and clue. Well planned murder. I tell you." I continuously said whatever I was thinking and then paused for a few minutes.

I continued *"But what after 3:40pm? He went back again to office just to come back home at 4:20pm? But why?"* I was interrupted by Sam *"Sir to be seen in CCTV that he came at 4:20pm not at 3:20pm... he knew about the CCTV right?"*

"Yeah you are right..." I replied.

"And sir according to his call record he called his wife at 3:00 pm may be to inform her that he is coming and Ana was ready to open the door upon hearing the bell" said Sam.

I continued "*So that he could enter the house while bus interrupts the camera's view...*" and after a two minutes pause I continued again "*But he could also have entered the house at 3:45 why only at 4:20 and could've called us at 3:50 pm.*"

"*Sir*" called Addy as he entered the room and continued "*He left office at 3:00pm.*"

"*That's it!!!*" I said taking a deep breath. Finally solving the case at 10:40pm.

And I continued *"He knew we would track his location just to fool us, he kept his phone somewhere in the office, came back home at 3:20 pm murdered his wife and left 3:40 pm to reach office at 4:00 again, took his phone and came back home. So that we may think that he was actually in the office"* I said and quickly continued "*And hired someone yesterday to snatch his brother-in-law's phone and kept it at his residence just to divert us to Brenden and make him the culprit where as he's the actual culprit.*"

Both Addy and Sam looked satisfied with my theory and now ready to arrest the actual culprit of the victim. Victim's husband himself. I nodded my head which they both understood that I meant '*Go and Arrest that Bastard*' as they left.

Addy and Sam were back soon in no time arresting Jose Thomson who tried his best to save himself and get away with hands full of his wife's blood.

***

"*Property... Her father had a big property built as an old house where no one lives now... right in middle of a commercial area on Corporate Road where I wanted to build a complex for a very long time. I offered him and tried to convince him but he always refused saying it belongs to his ancestors and he wants to keep it as their memory... What bull shit!!!... Memories of Dead ones are Useless... memories don't give us money or pay our bills.*" Jose confessing his crime.

"*Continue*" I said.

"*Just a year after that fortunately Ana's parents met with an accident and then I made this plan*" after a small pause he continued again "*I knew about the CCTV and the Buses timings stopping there, but I knew I would be the Main Suspect and also that you guys will check phone location... that's why I hired a thief to snatch Brenden's phone and kept it at my house and mine at the office... So that he would be accused and then I threw his phone in the bus*" confessed his crime and reason behind it.

I turned my face to Addy & Sam standing near the door. And they took Jose out of my eyes and probably locked him in to prison for life now.

***

***

'BEHIND EVERY CRIME THERE IS ALWAYS A REASON'

This is what I believe. Sometimes you get to know the possible reasons first which makes the case solve faster than usual. You eat food when you are hungry. You drink water because you are thirsty. Every action by Human has some reason behind it except reflex actions. So instead of finding who ate food find out who was hungry. Instead of finding who drank the water find out who was thirsty. You probably tend to find the answer to both in less time.

***

"*Here is your coffee mister*" said my wife Amanda – a school teacher, teaching mathematics at Amsteria National School, Indust Branch; as I just came out after taking a cool water bath under the shower.

"*Keep it on the table*" I replied her as I settled myself on my reading chair accompanied by a round table in our balcony surrounded by a couple of flower pots, a pleasant view of bright sun rising to make our day hotter and working under it tougher (laughing) and of course fresh air that makes up the mood. (Sipping Coffee) It's just a usual morning; waking up at 6 am, taking a cool water bath under the shower followed by a hot coffee while reading newspaper.

"*Breakfast is readyyy*" shouted my wife from the kitchen.

"*Yeahhh... mom.... cominggg...*" loudly responded our 10-years-old daughter, Andrea – a 3rd grade student, studying at Amsteria National School, Indust Branch. Same school where my wife works as a math teacher but they've set a rule that, In School they are just a teacher and a student.

"*Chaaddd*" shouted my wife to our son 6-years-old son Chadd – also a student but at Indust City Nursery School.

"*What's your brother doing*" asked Amanda to Andrea.

"*Still on bed mommm*" Andrea replied.

"*Charles, at least do me a favor by helping me to wake him up*" said my wife to me and she continued "*It's you who spoiled him.*"

"*Huh okay*" I replied as I went to their room.

"*Hey... Wake-up*" "*Chadd wake up now*" "*You gotta go to school.*"

"*Yeahh dad, just give me five more minutes*" he replied with his eyes closed.

"*Okay but just five minutes after that wake up yourself don't make me wake you again*" I said him; he reminds me of my childhood when even I wished to sleep a little more, a little five minutes more while my mom used to keep shouting on me.

"*Okayye Dad*" he replied & I left his room to change because he might have five more minutes but I don't.

"*Come on Charles breakfast is ready*" shouted my wife again.

Whenever I get ready for work, I feel committed to serve the nation and protect the people by solving the cases such as Robbery, Murder, kidnapping, Rape, Extortion, & etc. etc.... Some are committed in the broad day light and some are in the darkness of night. Some are caught on Cameras and some just by naked eyes. Some are committed in front of crowd and some in private. Some people witnesses the crime and some try to take some action. Some people help the culprits and some just mind their own business. Some people oppose the Victim and some just stay away from it. Some people come out as eye witnesses and some just deny their presence. But most importantly some Crimes are reported to us and some not even report.

***

Served breakfast myself and switched on the television.

(On the Television) '*Hey Pikaman, please help us*'

"*Hey!!! how many times should I say you guys to change the channel before switching it off*" I said to my children in an arrogant tone. These kids should start reading books (especially of SSMtypes) instead of watching cartoons.

Channel Change

(On the Television)

"*You ruined my life, my love, my dignity and today you'll have to payback for all that you've done to me. All of you wait for Sunday, Sunday is gonna be a red letter day*" said the guy in the video, holding a gun, wearing grey t-shirt; with a wheel and a tool box hanging on the wall in the background. Video continues followed by a female voice in the background "*Please leave me, please, I'm Sorry, I won't do it again, just leave me*" who seemed very scared.

(On the Television)

"*Who's this guy? What are his intentions? What's he talking about? Who's that girl behind him? What he actually wants? Why he sent us this Video? Does he have no faith in the Government? In the Police Department? Or in the Law?*" questioning, the anchor of the show. You know these news channel anchors; Their Job is to Report the Crime, share the news not to blame someone for it. They've no right to do. But who cares it all works like that. Sometimes they actually help a case to solve faster as this one.

"*Hey Momm where's my breakfast*" I heard my daughter coming towards the dining hall. (Channel Changed) because I don't want my daughter to know how evil the world actually is; I want her to stay away from such evilness, from evil eyes, evil people.

But that the same time I don't want her to see everyone in that way, I want her to respect and love everyone.

(Phone ringing)

Commissioner Sir Calling flashed my phone screen.

"Hello sir good morning" I wished him as soon as I picked his call.

"Bad morning officer, bad morning" He said sounding a bit disturbed.

"Why sir, is everything alright?" I asked him.

"Come to my office, I've an assignment for you" he replied.

"Okay sir, I'll be there in 20 minutes" I assured him and we ended the call.

(Calling Addison)

"Hello" I said as soon as he picked up the call.

"Hello sir, good morning" said Addison.

"Good morning, good morning" I replied and continued saying *"Addison come directly to the commissioner's office with Samuel, I'll also reach there directly."*

"Okay sir, we'll be there" replied Addison and we ended up the call.

Meanwhile I had my breakfast; "*Darling I am leaving*" I said to my wife while she was in the changing room.

"*Okay darling... bye*" she replied from inside the locked changing room.

"*Bye Study hard at school*" I said to Andrea & Chadd while they were having breakfast.

"*Bye dad... have a nice day at work*" replied Andrea as I kissed her on forehead.

(Smiling) "*Bye dad... and you too work hard*" replied my son as I also kissed him on forehead and lightly slapped him for his fun with dad. (Laughing)

***

As I entered the Commissioner's Office Premises – an old building used by ministers of King Williamson during his ruling period now turned into Police Commissioner's Office; there was a crowd of news media reporters and cameramen outside of the office questioning about the incident and demanding commissioner's comments on the same; the police officers trying to set them calm and asking them to leave. "*We'll call you guys whenever commissioner sir has to say anything*" said one police officer. This usually happens during such incidents and we are all used do it. Walking to the commissioner's cabin, passing by few cabins and wishing a number police officers; some seniors and some juniors.

(Knocking at Commissioner's Cabin)

"*Excuse Me sir*" I took his permission while he in his early 50's was on a phone call sitting on a big moveable and comfortable chair in front of a big round table with some books, files and papers all around the table and a name plate 'George Oliver' embraced in the middle; he noticed me and asked to come in.

(Commissioner on phone)

"*Yeah... sir... but... hmm... yeahh... yes sir... hmm... I'll hand it over to my best officer... oh okay... yes of course... you don't worry about it anymore... okay sir... Bye sir*" and he ended up the call.

"*Have you seen the News?*" he asked.

"*Yeah, I've seen*" I answered.

"*See, there is a lot of pressure from the high levels regarding this news; it has created a fuss in the nation, people are scared, and those news media persons are pointing out on security of women in the nation*" He said & continued after a pause "*You are the best we've got. I want you to handle this case now and solve it really quick & rescue the girl unharmed.*"

"*Sir, thank you, but we don't really know when & where that incident took place & when the video was actually recorded... I mean is that footage even legit or if it is then when was it recorded... maybe it's an old clip which went viral now*" I shared my doubts and continued after a second pause and silence "*Anyhow I'll look into it... you don't worry... I'll solve it soon... you don't worry.*"

"*That's what I expect from you Charles, you've full support from me and the department*" the commissioner assured me.

"*Okay sir...*" I said him as I left his cabin.

***

"*Good morning, sir!*" Addy and Sam wished me as they waited for me outside the commissioner's cabin.

"*Good morning... Good morning...*" I replied while we walked towards the exit.

"*Addy, let me know which news channel first broadcasted this news*" I ordered Addy while we were en-route to ICCB Headquarters – Our Office.

"*Sir, 24x7News Channel was the first to broadcast that video footage then followed by others*" answered Addy.

"*Take to 24x7News's Office then*" I ordered Sam who was driving our Car. This is the first time we are breaking our rule of not talking while driving to the office for the first time after we took over a case.

"*And Addy till then you contact other news channel and from where they got it*" I ordered Addy.

"*Okay, Sir*" replied Addy as he started making calls.

***

(24x7News Channel's Office – a fully equipped 10 floors glass building)

"*Hello, I'm Senior Officer Charles, Charles Beckett; SID, Crime Branch*" I said at the reception showing my ID to the lady at the reception in her early 20s wearing a professional suit with a simple watch on the right hand.

"*Hello sir, how may I assist you?*" asked the receptionist.

"*We want to meet Editor in Chief here*" I said.

"*Okay sir, let me check*" she replied and pressed a key on the landline and took the receiver.

(Receptionist on the phone) "*Hello sir, a Crime Branch Officer is here to meet you*" followed by "*Okay sir, okay*" & she kept down the receiver.

"*Come, follow me, sir*" she said and we started following her, passing by many small cabins and workspaces where everyone was busy on their own, some on computers, some on mobile phones, some writing on white boards, to some typing; passing by all these she took us to the Editor in Chief's cabin; the biggest of all as of till now we've passed by.

***

"*Sir... Senior Officer Charles from SID*" she introduced me to the Editor in Chief, standing in well-furnished and technology driven cabin; probably in his late 40's, you need to cross that age in order to be eligible for this position which requires long years of experience.

"*Yeah, nice to meet you*" wished the Editor in Chief and continued "*I'm Michael Eisner, Editor in Chief here*" he introduced himself.

"*You can leave now*" he said to the receptionist and she left.

"*Yeah tell me... how can I help you?*" he asked me.

"*I'm here to enquire about the news being broadcast on your channel since morning*" I asked him.

"*Yeah, tell me what you want to know?*" he replied.

"*Where did you get that clip?*" I questioned him.

"*Actually our camera man found it lying outside our office. It was a pen drive packed in an envelope*" he answered.

"*Camera man? Can we meet him?*" I said him.
"*Okay, of course*" he replied and took his phone.

(Michael on Phone)

"*Hello, Is James in the office?*" He asked on phone followed by "*Where he went? Oh... okay let me know when he's back*" he said & ended.

"*Sorry officer, he isn't in the Office, he went with a reporter to a news lead, and I guess he'll be back in some time*" he said.

"*Okay we'll wait; do you've that envelope?*" I asked.

"*Yeah of course... umm...*" he responded and went towards the drawer in the corner of the room at his side. "*Here it is*" he said as he handed me the envelope.

I looked and scrutinized the envelope there was no address or postal stamp on it but only IMPORTANT written in dark red, capital, bold letters; that means it was not posted through any courier, someone personally dropped the envelope there.

"*So how can you run a clip without even knowing about it?*" I questioned him.

"*What's there to know... we know it's a legit video recorded yesterday... That's enough*" he answered.

"*How can you be so sure that it was recorded yesterday*" I questioned him again.

"*See, officer... for every file the device automatically stores the date and time of when it was first created... and for videos that first creation date and time is recording date and time*" He explained.

"*Okay... hmm... so where did he find this?*" I asked.

"*Outside the office*" he replied.

"*Is there a CCTV Camera focusing that angle?*" I questioned him.

"*Yes of course we do*" he answered.

"*Okay then we would like to see today's morning footage*" saying this to Michael; I handed the envelope to Addy.

Michael took us to the Monitor room. "*What's the office timings?*" I asked.

"*We are open 24 hours but only a minimal staff works in the night shift...*" he replied.

"*So that cameraman is of which shift?*" I asked him.

"*Day Shift*" he replied.

"*So what are his timings?*" I asked.

"*9am to 4pm*" Michael replied.

"*And when the night shift staff leaves?*" I asked him.

"*They leave after the morning shift staff takes over... Mm... So around 9:15 to 9:30*" Michael replied.

"*Then play the footage from 8am*" I said Michael.

***

08:00:00:00 - showed the timing of the footage on screen.

08:01:04:17 – A few vehicles passing by on road.

08:07:09:43 – But No movement.

08:13:19:99 – In the Office Premises.

08:21:03:65 – Still No movement.

08:27:13:00 – A Sweeper comes in.

08:27:31:50 – Sweeper starts cleaning the floor.

08:31:43:09 – Still cleaning.

08:34:00:46 – Sweeper leaves.

08:39:42:23 – A guy wearing facemask, black hoody, jeans and black sneakers; moves in and places something on floor and leaves.

08:48:43:11 – Staff starts to come-in one-by-one.

08:53:25:34 – But no one notices it lying on the floor.

08:56:43:52 – The cameraman comes in, notices that thing and picks it up (probably that thing is envelope) and enters the office.

***

"*Hey you've watchmen at night as well right?*" I asked to Michael.

"*Okay, share his address, phone number and every detail with Addison*" I asked Michael.

"*And Addy, you call the watchman to Crime Branch Headquarters*" I ordered Addy.

"*Okay Sir*" replied Addy as he took out his phone to execute the task.

"*Show us the footage from another angle*" I said to Michael.

"*May be we can get some clue*" I said to everyone in the room. Footage from another angle had no extra information and no clue to reach that anonymous guy.

"*Michael, give us the copy of the footages & Thanks for co-operating with us*" I said to Michael.

"*That's my responsibility Officer*" he replied and copied the footage to a disk and handed it over to me and continued "*but I need a favor from you.*"

"*What kind of favor?*" I asked.

"*Can you give us an interview regarding this case*" he offered.

"*Oh I see, actually Michael we just started investigating, so I've nothing much to share, but don't worry I'll definitely give one when I reach up to some extent then we'll have something to share and some detailed information*" I replied him and continued "*After all, who doesn't want to be seen on television*" I joked smiling.

"(Laughing) *Yeah, right, see you soon then*" replied Michael.

"*And whenever the camera-man comes ask him to meet me at the headquarters*" I said to Michael and continued after a pause "*Actually... do one thing... share his address, phone number and every detail you've about him with Addison.*"

"*Okay, of course*" he replied as I & Michael shook hands and we left the office.

***

"*Addy, make photo copies of that guy from the video & circulate his picture to all the police stations and ask them search for him and also check him in the police records; maybe he might've committed some crime in the past*" I said to Addy while driving back to headquarters.

"*Okay sir*" replied Addy.

"*And Sam get me the details about all the missing reports filed in this week*" I ordered Sam.

"*Okay sir*" replied Sam.

After reaching the station I started watching the viral clip again, in hope of finding some clue.

Play. "*You ruined my life, my love, my dignity and today you'll have to payback for all that you've done to me. All of you wait for Sunday, Sunday is gonna be a red letter day*" said the guy in the video, holding a gun, wearing grey t-shirt; with a wheel and a tool box hanging on the wall in the background.

Pause. Umm... She ruined his life?

Play. A female voice in the background "*Please leave me, please, I'm Sorry, I won't do it again, just leave me*" who seemed very scared.

Pause. As I saw the video again and again repeatedly for a couple of times hoping that I would get some clue but no luck. Every time I watch, I just get more confused. About who is this guy? What he wants? What's actually happening? Till now I've just understood, that the girl, whoever she is, has done something wrong to this guy and now, he's taking revenge. So who's the actual Victim, the guy or the girl? Umm... May be there is some case registered accusing that girl we need to tally the missing complaints of females with case registered accusing females.

"*Sir here are all the missing reports filed this week*" Sam said handing over me the file.

I opened it.

Total 129 Missing Complaints

Aaron Kidman – age 13.......

Ab.......

Abraham – age 58.........

Belinda – Age: 23 – Missing Since: 4 days – Wearing: White t-shirt and pink pants – Last Seen: 10:50 pm leaving Century Club after a party with friends.

Frank – Age: 8.......

Harman – Age: 57..........

Malcolm – Age: 22..........

Nuts – Age: 10....

Oliver – Age: 07.........

Racheal – Age: 15 – Missing Since: 13 days – Wearing: White t-shirt and pink pants – Last Seen: 2:05pm; returning back from college, Tietan, Indust City.

Samantha Sead – Age: 12 – Missing Since: 13 days – Wearing: White t-shirt and pink pants – Last Seen: 5:20pm playing at Newton Colony Park, Newton Colony, Sector 09, Alphasphere, Indust City.

Tasha – Age: 09.......

Yoko....

Zac...

"*This won't work... we need to have some clue*" I said and continued "*Sam, also get me all the cases filed accusing a female*" I ordered Sam.

"*Okay sir*" Sam accepted and left. As Crompton left, I was thinking about what case could be registered accusing a female. By her voice she seemed to be in her mid-twenties, what crime could such a young lady commit?? Murdered his loved or closed ones? May be his parents? Or maybe they both were in love and she cheated? Or they were married? Answer to all this questions lies in the guy's or the girl's identity and all these thoughts running through my head ended as Addy entered with a guy wearing a plain light colored shirt and dark colored pant with a pair of sandal, I guessed it's the watchman.

"*Sir, this is the watchman*" Addy said as he entered my cabin along with him.

"*What's your name*" I asked the watchman.

"*Edgar*" he responded.

"*So Edgar, a random guy who came into the 24x7 News Channel Office during your working time... why didn't you stop him*" I questioned him.

"*That's impossible, no one unknown came inside the office*" he answered and before I could say anything he continued "*Can you tell me the timing?*" he asked.

"*Around 8:30am*" I replied him and he went onto think.

"*Only the sweeper comes around that time*" he replied and quickly continued "*But he only sweeps outside, not inside.*"

"*Yeah but doesn't that comes under your office premises*" I said and waited for his answer but he didn't give one. So I continued "*A guy came near the building entrance and dropped something*" I said him.

"*Who?*" he said and was very quick to continue "*Sorry sir, I sit inside the building and from there I don't have any idea of what happens outside*" he replied.

"*Your job is to keep an eye on the entire office premises not just inside... what if someone drops a bomb or someone gets murdered outside the office*" I scolded him and he wasn't able respond.

"*Okay... but from next time, be cautious*" I said him in a disappointed tone, he nodded his head wanting to say okay. Addy showed him the way to exit, he left and Addy stayed.

"*Cameraman turned up?*" I asked Addy.

"*No sir, he isn't picking up the call*" he replied.

"*Call Michael and enquire about him*" I ordered him and before he could make a call, I continued "*What about the guy in the footage? Any information from our records or elsewhere?*"

"*No sir, he's not in our records and I've circulated his picture, local police are searching for him*" he replied to which I nodded my head, in reply.

(Addison on call) "*Hey Michael*" he said and continued "*I'm Addison calling from SID Crime Branch*" followed by "*So the cameraman come to the office?*" "*Ohh*" "*Ask him to visit us*" it seems he's in the office, "*Okay*" he ended the call.

"*Sir he is in the office; I've asked him to come here*" Addy said as soon as he ended up the call.

"*Okay*" I replied.

Six & half hours passed since we took up this case but we are still clueless. Not even a single evidence that can make the case move forward.

***

(Phone ringing)

Commissioner Sir Calling flashed my phone screen.

A call from Commissioner Sir was ringing on my phone and I had to pick up but didn't know what to say, still I ended up picking his call.

"Hello sir" I wished him as soon as I received his call.

"Hello, any updates?" he asked me.

"Not much sir, we are on it… you don't worry" I assured him.

"Okay but put your best in this case… and let me know if you need any kind of help" he replied offering me help.

"No sir, I'll do it… as soon as possible… you just relax" I assured him.

"Yes that's why I handed over this case to you" he said and continued *"The news is still running up all over the news channels in the entire nation and has been trending all over the internet, since morning."*

"Yes sir, I know" I replied and continued after a pause *"I'll end it soon."*

"Okay" he replied and ended up the call.

This news made the entire nation question about their safety and security to the police department and government. Hey, wait commissioner sir actually helped me. Entire nation. We've been searching for the guy only in our city were as we should do it all over the nation.

***

I called Addy.

"*Hello*" I said as he received the call.

"*Hello, sir*" he replied and quickly continued "*Sir James, the cameraman has come over. I am bringing him to you.*"

"*Okay*" I replied him and ended the call.

***

James, a nerdy type guy wearing sunglasses and formals, he seemed little nervous.

"*Hello James*" I said him as he along with Addy entered the cabin.

"*Hello sir*" he replied and continued after a minute of silence in the room "*Why I'm called here?*" he asked.

"*We would like to know about that footage running on news channel you work for*" I asked him.

"*I don't know anything about it*" he replied in a nervous tone. Making his way to my suspect list now.

"*Wasn't it you who found that clip?*" I questioned him.

"*I just found it lying outside the office*" he replied.

"*How come only you found that whereas no one else did?*" I questioned him again.

"*Maybe because I'm a quick observant*" he replied.

"*Ohh okay... You see anyone keeping it over there? Or anyone there doubtful*" I asked him.

"*No, no one like that... just a few staff members entering*" he replied. Now making way for himself to the top in my suspects list. May be he's the second culprit after that guy in the video, or maybe he's the one behind it.

"*Anything else you would like to share with us or you think we should know*" I asked him to which he shortly replied "*No, nothing.*"

"*Okay then... we'll call you upon need*" I said him and shook hands as he left leaving Addy and Me in the Cabin.

***

"*He's my prime suspect now*" I said to Addy.

"*Even I suspect him*" he replied.

And just then Sam came in "*Sir here are all the cases registered accusing women*" he said as he handed over the file to me and continued "*And that guy is nowhere in the city... all the police station units searched for him.*"

I handed over the file to them and ordered "*Tally this with the missing complaints of females*" followed by few minutes of silence and sounds of turning pages, which ended as Sam spoke "*Sir, No Match*" and followed by silence in the room again.

"*To solve this case we need to know the guy's identity and that won't happen if we search for him only in our city. We should search for him nationwide. Each and every City of Unistan*" After a pause "*Call Joseph back & the top 16 officers of our branch*" I ordered and continued "*I want all of them in my cabin in 30 minutes.*"

"*Make four team amongst yourselves*" I ordered our top 16 officers and they divided themselves into four teams, with four in each.

"*Where's Joseph?*" I enquired.

"*Sorry Sir, here I am*" replied Joseph himself as he entered the Cabin.

"*Is it okay to come back*" I asked him to which he replied "*It's my duty Sir!*"

"*Good*" I appreciated him and after a minute pause I continued "*Addison, Samuel, Joseph & I would lead each team operating north, south, east and west zones of the nation. I'll take northern zone… Addy, you take southern… Sam you take western… and Jos you take eastern zone*" after a minute pause and mumbling in the cabin I continued again "*You all know the present situation… it's spreading like a fire and our department is, soo much in pressure. Moreover, It's about public safety and we need to solve it asap*" I continuously said without any pause.

"*We are ready Sir*" everyone in the cabin said with full of energy and motivation.

"*Good*" I replied with a nodding head as we departed for our respective destinations.

***

We landed at Aslansa Airport – the city; my first destination in the northern zone. And went straight to Aslansa Police Headquarters.

"*Hello sir, we were informed that you are coming*" said an officer opening the door for us and continued as we walked in into the headquarters "*This way sir*" showing us the way to our temporary cabin.

Wasting no time in introduction, "*Hey, get us the record of all the kidnapping cases and cases accusing a female solved & unsolved; all*" I ordered the officer who welcomed us to his office.

"*Here it is*" he said as he kept a stack of files on the table.

"*Two of you tally the details of females kidnapped with the cases accusing a female. And let me know if there's any match*" I ordered them and continued "*And you two*" pointing at the remaining two officers from my team and seeing at the Aslansa Police Officer; Name batch on his chest says Alex "*And also you... Come with me we need to search for the guy with his picture all around the city*" I ordered and after a quick pause I continued "*But before that you officer, check that guy if he's there in any of the police records*" I ordered Alex.

"*No sir he is not in our records*" said Alex as he came after 20 minutes while we were helping officers who were tallying the records which resulted in No Matches Found. "*Call Addy, Sam & Jos and ask them what are they up to?*" I ordered to one of my team members.

After spending hours, asking peoples, roaming kilometers, searching for the guy and still not finding anything was frustrating us. "*Sir, Addy, Sam & Jos none of them had any news or update*" said my officer while we were going to BM Hills, last area left here in the City of Aslansa.

"*Have you ever seen this guy?*" we questioned the guy at the counter of Alman Café in BM Hills. He looked through the photo for a minute and finally we heard something we were dying to hear since last few hours "*Yes.*"

"*When? Where?*" I questioned him to which he answered "*Many times, here at the café, he is our regular customer.*"

"*Who is he? Where is he now?*" I questioned him again.

"*He's Victor, he usually visits with his girlfriend, Amelia*" he answered and continued after a pause "*I haven't seen him for a month, now. Except on television since morning*" sounding disappointed and shocked with such a behavior from one of his regular customers.

"*Didn't you feel like to inform police that you know him?*" I questioned him.

"*Sorry sir, actually I thought you guys know his identity*" he answered.

"*Have you ever found something weird about him? Or any such suspicious behavior or incident?*" asked one of my team members to which he quickly replied "*Last time, when he visited along with his girlfriend Amelia, suddenly in middle of having of coffee Amelia left and he tried to stop her... nothing other than that... in fact I could say he's one of our understanding customers. And I totally don't understand why he is doing that...*"

"*Let us know everything you remember about him*" said my team member.

"*Nothing more... that's all I knew*" he replied.

"*Do you know his address?*" I asked him.

"*Yes, he's son of Mr. Cedric Quentin, lives down the street in one of the lavish villas over there.*"

"*What Mr. Cedric does?*" I questioned him.

"*He is MD of Quentin Associates*" he replied and after a quick pause continued "*That's all I know.*"

And he went on to attend his customers as we left.

We searched for Mr. Cedric's house and after passing by a few villas we found a villa named 'Quentin Villa' followed by name plate 'Quentin Associates'. We went to the gate and a watchman there stopped us.

"*What brings you here? No one is home*" he lied as I could see lights on in the villa and moreover it's 11:00am now.

"*We are Police*" said Alex showing his ID.

"*Sorry sir, Mr. Cedric Sir asked me not to allow anyone*" he replied.

"*Open the gate*" Alex ordered him.

We went in and entered the house. A man in black colored three-piece suit came annoyed to us, "*Who let you in? What you want*" he shouted.

"*Police*" said Alex showing his ID to him too.

"*Is he your son?*" my team member asked him showing Victor's photo copy.

"*Unfortunately yes*" he replied.

"*Unfortunately?*" I asked him.

"*Yes unfortunately… it's my bad luck to have a son like him*" he replied with anger clearly visible on his face and continued "*He's now a criminal you can do whatever you want with him.*"

A lady came running from inside with tears in her eyes and sadness on her face "*What the hell are you saying? He is our son damn it... for god sake keep your mouth shut*" shouted the lady on Cedric, possibly his wife.

"*Where's my son?*" asked the lady to us.

"*We are here to ask you the same*" I replied her.

"*Ask us? Even we don't know about him*" she replied, confused.

"*Didn't you arrest him?*" asked Cedric.

"*No we didn't, his identity was not known until now*" Alex replied him.

"*Why you guys are here then?*" he confusedly asked.

"*What why? What do you mean by that?*" I said and quickly continued "*He is nationally known criminal now, who's still roaming around freely*"

"*So what you want from us?*" he asked again, while his wife is just listening to us.

"*Why he's doing such crime?*" I questioned seeing both Cedric and his wife.

"*How are we supposed to know?*" replied Cedric.

"*We don't know why he's doing like this, but trust me, he was never such a guy. He, always, was a well-mannered, caring and loving person. Good at studies, so also at sports*" replied his mother as tears rolled down her cheeks.

Whatever they said till now it is clear that they don't know where he is. "*When he was last seen?*" I asked them.

"*About a month ago*" replied his mother. The employ at the Alman Café also said the same.

"*Any change in his behavior during that time or before he disappeared?*" I asked them and before they could reply, I continued "anything suspicious?"

"*Yes, week before he disappeared...*" said his mother but was quickly interrupted by his father Cedric "*What you are talking that's different and this is different!*"

"*We need to know everything Mr. Cedric*" I said him to which he replied after a pause "*Nothing... she was just saying about his break up.*" Even that guy said about the girlfriend leaving him.

I doubt the voice of a girl in the video is of his girlfriend. "*Where's his girlfriend now?*" I asked them.

"*We don't know*" they replied.

"*Okay do you've her phone number or any sort of details so we can reach her?*" I asked them again to which his mother replied "*She studies in the same college as Victor does, Micro College of Management, you'll find her there.*"

"*Hmm... okay... can we've look at Victor's Room*" I asked.

"*Okay*" she replied as Cedric went to sofa and sat and she took us to the Victor's room.

"*Search everywhere*" I ordered my team and they started searching everywhere. Victor's room was full of posters of football players. He seemed to be a football lover. As I was going through the posters his mother said "*He was very good at football and captain of his school team*" in reply I nodded my head.

"*Sir...*" called one of my team members showing me a diary to me, probably Victor's. I asked him to keep it with us.

"*Please don't harm my son... he is not like that*" said Victor's mother.

"*Yeah don't worry... I understand*" I replied as I left their house.

It's nearly 12:00am now, everyone looks sleepy and tired. "*Let's end now but be early in the morning*" I ordered everyone as we reached the station.

"*Sir we've a Guest house you can stay there*" Alex offered me.

"*No I'm okay here*" I replied him pointing at the cabin.

"*Are you sure sir?*" he asked me.

"*Yes*" I replied.

"*If you need anything there's a constable here for you*" he informed me to which I replied "*Okay*"

I sat on chair with not so sleepy eyes, thinking only about the case. The first case in my history that is taking me so long to solve. From the dawn to the mid of night, we've only been able to find the guy's identity. And doubt that the female voice in the video is of his girlfriend. Now this case looks simple.

(Phone Ringing)

Mastermind Calling flashed my phone screen.

Mastermind? Why is he calling me? I'm blessed and lucky to get a call from mastermind himself but at the same time I'm confused. I mean Mastermind; Unistan Secret Force's best man; who was given the title of 'Mastermind' by his seniors. He's the secret government wants no one to know. Uniquely Trained and highly Motivated. There's no secret he cannot extract, no security he cannot breach, no person he cannot become. I took his number when I met him last year at commissioner's party thinking that in some important and crucial time I'd call him. But never ever thought he'd call me.

All these thoughts ended as I received his call.

"Hello Sir" I said as I picked up his call.

"Hello Charles" he replied.

"Yes sir… I'm feeling so lucky that you called" I expressed my gratitude to him and continued *"What can I do for you?"*

"Yeah do me a favor, buy yourself a new pair of shoe" he replied.

"Sorry? Shoes for myself? But why?" I replied confusedly.

"Do it" he replied and ended the call before I could ask him anything more.

I don't want to call him back; I would look stupid if I do. Let's go to buy one then. As soon as I went outside the cabin, a constable came running to me, "*Can I do anything for you? Sir*" he asked me. The name batch on his chest says 'Ronald'. "*Yeah*" I replied him as we walked outside the office together and I continued "*Take me to the nearest shoe store*" I said him as we went to jeep, sat in and left.

"*Dark Brown Formal*" I said to the helper at the shoe store and continued "*size 8*" That's my usual choice. He walked by a few steps, took out a box and shoes out of it.

"*Here it is*" said he as he kept them in front of me. I picked them up searching for any clue in there. But I found nothing but in return a 'Is he stupid' look from the helper and Ronald. I removed the same pair of shoe I was wearing, put my legs in the new ones. Not much difference and also found no clue. May be he was playing a prank with me. Anyhow I'll buy this one, just to be optimistic, that it might help me in solving this case, which made me spend night in police headquarters of Aslansa.

"*Pack them*" I said to the helper who was staring at me. I know Ronald would be confused with me, already having a good pair of shoe but buying a new and that too at this point of time, all of sudden. But trust Me, I'm confused myself, firstly this case and now Mastermind and his wish for me to get a new pair of shoe for myself.

All these thoughts ended as we reached the station. I stepped out of the jeep, went in to the cabin, sat on the chair accompanied by a big square but curved edged table; confused and thinking about the shoe. which ended again as I noticed evidence bag on the table. I took the bag, picked out his personal diary from it and started reading it. May be I could find some clue or something.

I went straight to the last page.

Dated 06/04/2017:

'I've decided to take revenge'

Written in capital bold letters. So possibly on or after this day only he committed the crime of kidnaping, now this will make easy to find the girl, we can search for unsolved kidnapping cases on and after this date, 06/04/2017.

I turned back a page.

Dated 01/04/2017:

'I confessed everything to my parents thinking they really care. But they said "Forget about it, don't reveal it to anyone… what'll our society think? Please don't bring down our family's name and respect in the society." But they cared more about the family's name and respect in the society and how can I forget thattt.'

I turned back one more page.

Dated 31/03/2017:

'I confessed it to Amelia thinking she really loved me. But she said "I can't be with such a guy who was...." and left me alone in the café while I was begging her not to leave, I hope my parents would understand me, they really care about me, I'm sure at least they'll understand me and help me.'

I turned back another page hoping he might have mentioned about what he is talking about here and in the video.

Dated 30/03/2017:

'I confessed about it Barry & Nigel thinking they are my really friends. They said "We can't be friends with such a loser; you've no place for our friendship now." But weren't my real friends. I think I should share this with Amelia, I'm sure she would understand me.'

I turned back another page once again.

Dated 29/03/2017:

'I'm broken, teared and everything worst that can happen to a human. I've never thought about it even in my horror dreams, I think I should share about this with Nigel and Barry, they are my real friends and I'm sure they would understand me and help me.'

Now I think it's clear that the voice in the clip was not of Amelia's but anyhow we should meet her and Victor's friends, and parents again and ask them what he confessed. I turned back another page again this time too hoping he might have mentioned what exactly happened to him.

Dated 08/11/2016:

'She acceptedddd… Finally, I proposed her at city's most popular five-star Restaurant & Hotel Alman.'

I think this is before the tragedy and its waste if I read any further. I closed his diary and kept it back in the evidence bag. What actually happened with him? And why is he doing this now? Unable to crack the reason behind the crime is very frustrating for me. Why hadn't Addy or Sam or Jos updated me yet?

Let's call Addy.

(Called Addy)

"Helloww, Speedy Investigation Department, Officer Addison here" said Addy as soon as he received my call, with his voice I could make out that he was sleeping and that made me more furious. How could he sleep with an unsolved case whereas I'm feeling sleepless?

"Addison, Charles here" I replied him in a heavy tone.

"Sir… Sir… Sorry Sir" he replied.

"Didn't you think of calling and updating me" I scolded him.

"Sorry sir" he apologized and continued *"I, Sam and Jos have got nothing to share sir."*

"Hmm…" I replied and continued after a quick pause *"I've found the Guy's Identity. He's Victor Quentin s/o Mr. Cedric Quentin, an Aslansa based businessman."*

"That's great sir now it would be easy to solve this case" he replied in a satisfying tone.

"Nope, it isn't that easy as it seems, he's still roaming, we don't where he is… not the reason" I said disappointedly and continued *"Main thing is that the girl is still with him and he said he would take the real revenge Sunday, we should get her out of it before he does anything and for that we've only a day left"* followed by a two minute of silence.

"But Addy I got to knew the date when he committed himself to commit the crime" I said him and quickly continued *"06/04/2017"*

"That's great sir we need to see on kidnapping cases registered on and after 06/04" he replied with a hopeful voice.

"Yeah but we can make it easier" I said and quickly continued *"I read his personal diary and now I can say that everything was okay with him till 08/11… so what every happened was only between 08/11 and 19/05… so now what we got to do is… is to find out where he went in between that period… that is 08/11 to 19/05 and then we would for search kidnapping cases registered on and after 06/04, in those particular places."*

"Yes sir, searching for girl with filtering places Victor visited between 08/11 and 19/05 and then filtering kidnapping cases registered on or after 06/04 in those particular places would result in less cases and it would be easy for us to find out the victim" said Addy.

"Yes exactly" I replied him and continued *"But Addy, we don't know who the actual Victim is"* to which Addy replied with just hmm.

"Okay then I'll call you tomorrow" I said him.

"Waiting sir" he replied.

I continued *"Update all of this with Sam and Jos too"*

He replied again *"Okay sir"* followed by Bye from both the sides as we ended the call.

"*Good morning, sir!*" wished Alex as I opened my eyes from sleep at 8:13am. Alex and my team members were waiting for me to wake up. I was thinking about the case and don't exactly remember when I fell asleep, after a phone call with Addy which ended at 2:48 am.

"*Good morning*" I wished him back and continued "*Alex ask Victor's parents to the come here by 11:00 am and let's go to Victor's College now*" I said as I went to freshen up.

***

Reached Victor's college MCM. We went straight to the Administrative Office. "*Police*" Alex said showing his ID, he seems in no mood to introduce himself.

Alex continued "*We would like to meet Amelia, Barry and Nigel.*"

"*Sure sir*" replied the man who was sitting on the desk, now standing and continued "*Just a minute*" as he picked up the receiver of the landline and pressed a key.

"*Send Amelia, Barry and Nigel*" said he on the phone. Soon three of them were in the office.

***

I asked Amelia and Nigel to wait there and went outside in the open with Barry.

"*What do you think about Victor?*" I questioned him.

To which he quickly answered "*I don't know much about him, we are just classmates.*"

"*I've read his personal diary*" I said him.

"*Sorry, we were friends before but I don't have anything do with what he is doing*" he replied.

"*Don't worry about that we know you've nothing to do with it*" I assured him and questioned him "*When you last met him?*"

"*May be about two weeks ago*" he answered.

"*How was his behavior that day?*" I questioned him again.

He answered "*Normal just as usual.*"

And I again questioned him "*What did he say you that day?*"

"*Nothing we were just hanging out*" he quickly replied.

I reminded him again "*I said I read his personal diary.*"

To which he responded "*then you must already know everything why are you asking me?*"

"*He didn't mention what he said*" I said him.

After a minute pause he replied again, "*He said that he has cheated on Amelia during his 'visit to Indust.*"

"*Indust?*" I asked him and before he could respond I enquired "*Where else he visited?*"

"*He said me only about Indust*" he responded.

"*And was that the only reason you broke your?*" I asked him.

"*Yes, Amelia is like our sister, we can't bare someone cheating on her*" he replied.

***

I interrogated Amelia and Nigel after him. All three of them made almost the same statements. They all said that they broke their relation with him because he cheated on Amelia.

So now we've both the filters ready. I called Addy.

"*Hello*" I said as soon as he received the call.

"*Yes sir*" he replied.

"*Take the next flight back to Indust, our first filter is Indust*" to which he replied "*Okay sir*" as we ended the call.

We left the college. "*Book us the next flight to Indust*" I ordered one of my officers while we were en-route to Aslansa Police Headquarters.

Mr. Cedric Quentin was already waiting for me at the station. I asked them to come inside and have a seat.

"*I've read your child's personal diary*" I said them.

"*Okay so?*" replied Mr. Cedric.

"*So... I know that during his last conversation with you he confessed something*" I said them before any of them could say a word I continued "*What was it?*"

"*We already said you*" Cedric replied while his wife was just sitting beside him with a crying face seems like Cedric asked her not to speak anything.

Cedric continued "*He shared about his breakup with his girlfriend.*"

I asked "*What he said?*" seeing only Victor's mother now.

"*Exactly what Cedric said you now*" she replied.

"*Did he go anywhere in last few months? Any trip outside the city?*" I asked them.

To which now Cedric's wife replied "*Few months back he made a visit to Indust city.*"

"*Okay... and anywhere else*" I asked her.

"*Nope*" she made a quick reply.

I think it's waste to interrogate them anymore, Cedric is stubborn, he won't utter a single word and nor will let his wife do so.

"*Okay you can leave*" I said them and continued as we stood up from the table "*But you can't leave the city until this case is solved.*"

"*Solve it quickly then*" replied Cedric as they left the cabin.

"*Sir I doubt on Mr. Cedric that he is behind all this*" said an officer from my team.

"*No*" I quickly replied and continued "*he is just saving his fame in the society over his son.*"

"*Sir, we're to board a flight in next 30 minutes*" said the officer whom I asked to book us flight back to Indust.

"*Okay then let's leave*" I said them as we all walked outside the station.

"*Thanks for your amiability*" I said to Alex as we shook hands.

"*It's my pleasure and duty sir*" he replied. In no time we left the city of Aslansa, it was good working with the local cops here.

***

"*Welcome sir*" wished Addy and Sam as we reached Indust Airport "*Sir we filtered the search and it resulted in only 3 cases*" said Addy as we sat in the jeep.

"*Great*" I replied as he handed over the file to me.

I opened it.

Belinda – Age: 23 – Missing Since: 4 days – Wearing: White t-shirt and pink pants – Last Seen: 10:50 pm leaving Century Club after a party with friends.

Racheal – Age: 14.......

Samantha Sead – Age: 12.......

"*Belinda*" I said.

"*She was last seen with her friends at a party and went missing while she was returning home*" said Addy.

"*Let's go to see her parents first*" I ordered.

We went to Belinda's house. "*Yes?*" asked an elderly lady who opened the door for us.

"*Police*" said Sam showing his ID. The juniors always have the duty to introduce ourselves as Cops to the people who don't know us.

"*Ma'am*" she shouted for someone. May be she is the helper here, not the owner.

Another lady came from inside, "*What happened?*" she asked as she reached to us.

"*We are here to enquire about Belinda*" I said her.

"*Did you find her?*" she questioned me and before I could answer her, she continued "*How is she? Where is she now?*"

"*I'm sorry but we are still searching for her*" I answered making her disappointed and I continued "*for which we need your help.*"

"*Yes definitely*" she replied.

"*Call her friends here now*" I asked them.

"*Okay*" she replied as she started making calls.

After she was done with the calls I continued "*Do you know anyone named Victor? Or doubt your daughter would know?*"

"*No, I don't know anyone with that name*" she replied.

I questioned again "*Did she ever share anything related or about Aslansa?*" To which she replied again "*No, she never*" and continued "*Why would she discuss about a place where neither she nor we have been. And what it has to do with her gone missing?*"

"*We're just doing our job*" I replied and quickly questioned "*What about any boyfriend?*"

"*She never shared anything of that sort*" her mother replied as she started crying over her missing daughter and said "*I hope she won't get into any sort of problem like that News Clip.*"

Listening to this Me, Addy & Sam exchanged looks. Who would tell her that we doubt that she is the one in the video. But we are not sure yet so we can't share this with her mom.

Soon her friends showed up. I asked them same questions "*Do you know anyone named Victor? Or doubt your friend would know?*"

"*No, we don't know anyone with that name*" they replied.

How come no one knew Victor while he kidnapped their friend and her daughter. There is definitely a connection between Victor & Belinda which they really don't know or they are just hiding from us.

"*Did she ever share anything related or about Aslansa?*" I questioned the same to Belinda friends to which they gave a short and simple answer "*No*"

"*Do she have any boyfriend?*" I questioned them to which they hesitated to answer, may be because Belinda's mother was there.

"*You need to tell me that here or in-private*" I offered them.

But they replied there itself "*Yes she had boyfriends in the past but was currently single*" Knowing that I thought maybe Victor was her ex. But Victor had a girlfriend back in his city, Aslansa.

"*Any of her boyfriend was from Aslansa?*" I questioned.

"*No, I think*" replied one of her friends. This is weird; no connection then why would Victor kidnap her, a total stranger. Or maybe we are doubting on a wrong girl.

"*Where you all went for the last time with her?*"

"*At our mutual friend's birthday party at Century Club*" her friend replied. Century Club; that's an expensive club in the city.

"*Okay you can leave we'll call you upon need*" I said the girls as they left Belinda's house.

"*We'll take leave and will inform you as soon as we find something*" I said to Belinda's mother who was crying all the while, till then.

"*Please find her as early as possible*" he requested us.

"*I promise she'll be safe soon*" I assured her as we left the place.

"*Let's go to Century Club*" I said as soon as we entered the jeep.

***

Century Club playing music at high volume; which made us to talk louder than usual. "*Police*" said Sam to the bartender at the club showing his ID.

And this time before the bartender could ask how can he help us I said "*Call the manager*"

He went inside the cabin with 'OFFICE' written on its door just to come back in a minute along with a man in black suit, I suppose he is the Manager. As he came closer I could notice the 'Manager' batch on his chest.

"*How may I help you?*" asked the Manager.

We need to see the CCTV footages of 06/04/2017 after 11 am. We went to the Operator Room. Manager asked the Operator to play the clip of 06/04/2017 after 11 am.

He played. We were able to find Belinda in the video but not Victor. We tried every different angle but no, Victor wasn't here.

"*Play the outside one*" I said to the operator. The CCTV outside the club can only show Belinda and her friends leaving fully drunk and it ended with them walking out of focus and then out of the CCTV reach. And Victor was nowhere. We left the club.

"*Search if there are any CCTVs in the direction Belinda and her friends where walking*" I ordered Addy and Sam. But I too went along, we walked a few kilometers in every possible way but could not find any CCTV camera. I think the voice in the video was not of Belinda. We went back to the Club entrance where our jeep was parked.

***

Reached our office, disappointed, that the biggest clue we thought was not even a small one but don't know why somewhere inside I still felt there's a connection between Victor and Belinda.

As I went to my cabin I suddenly recalled Mastermind's Call and his wish for me to get a pair of shoe for myself. As I sat on my chair a sudden thought hit my head. He asked me to buy a pair of shoes but he didn't mention which one. And what I did? I bought the same one I usually wear.

"*Sam... Addy*" I shouted their names to call them here.

"*What happened sir*" asked both as they came in, running.

"*Play the 24x7 News Clip*" I ordered Sam and he quickly acted.

"*Go directly to where that unidentified guy kept the pen drive on floor*" I ordered as he fast forwarded the clip.

"*Zoom in to his shoes*" I ordered him again.

He zoomed in, a black color sneaker with two white lines in front and the sole outlined with white color.

"*Save this image*" I ordered and quickly continued "*And now start playing from the time staff starting coming in.*"

First Person. Footwear Not Matched.

Second Person. Footwear Not Matched.

Third Person. Footwear Not Matched.

Fourth Person. Footwear Not Matched.

Fifth Person. Footwear Not Matched.

Sixth Person. Footwear Matched.

Shit! It's James, the cameraman, he picked the pen drive which no one noticed because he was the one who kept it there. Mastermind is really mastermind, things which usually get unnoticed by everyone, he notices it.

"*Get him*" I ordered.

***

"*We know you kept it there*" I said to James who was sitting right in front of me, after Sam & Addy brought him here from his house, I'm sure he understood.

I continued "*Don't waste any more time.*"

He started crying and said "*I'm Sorry*" and after a minute of pause, he continued "*He made my house and family his hostage and threatened me if I don't make that clip run on channels then he would kill us.*"

And after a brief 5 minute of pause and silence in the room, he said *"I've nothing to do with him."*

"You could've shared that with us, we would've helped you" I said him to which he replied *"Sir, I've a 4-year-old son, I can't risk his life."*

I am a parent myself and I can understand his situation.

"So that garage is of your house" I asked him.

"Yes" he shortly replied.

"Where is he now?" I asked him.

"There only" he replied.

"Then how come Addy & Sam didn't notice him when they came to arrest you?" I asked.

"He was hidden in the garage" he replied.

"How many of people is with him?" I asked him.

"He is alone" he replied.

"And how many weapons?" I asked to which he replied *"Many."*

So now finally we've solved the case, *"Ask everyone to be ready to catch him"* I ordered. But I'm still a bit disappointed because I'm still unable to find the Reason behind the Crime. The first case that doesn't goes with my principle. Let's ask the culprit himself.

"*We are ready sir*" Sam said.

"*You wait here*" I said to James as I left the office to arrest Victor.

We reached there with arms ready, bullets loaded, eyes moving to every angle, and walking slowly without making noise.

"*You four wait here... outside*" I ordered to Addy, Sam and two other officers.

Three more officers with me to go in from the backside. We went inside James's house, we went in the direction of garage walking extra slow and quitter now.

We reached the Garage entrance from inside the house. We waited there for a minute, tried to hear any noise from inside to assume the movement but just got silence to hear.

"*Kick the door*" I mumbled to the officer beside me. He kicked the door as we were hiding.

"*Sir*" called the officer who kicked the door.

We went in. Victor was nowhere. Belinda along with a lady and a little kid were tied to the chairs in the middle and tape on their mouths. Victor ran away.

"*As your officers left arresting James, Victor ran away taking all his weapons with him*" said the lady, probably James's wife as we set them free.

The case is solved, we saved the girl, but culprit escaped. First case in my career history that I wasn't able to catch the culprit, but surely will catch him now.

***

"*Inform road, railway, air transport departments, send them Victor's picture*" I ordered my team as we sat in jeep and continued "*Addy, you stay here and take Belinda's confession and drop her home.*"

"*Put entire department on high alert, we've to get him...*" I shouted out of anger and quickly continued "*I want High Security at Airport, Railways, toll booths, and at every traffic signal... check each and every vehicle, leave no car, no bike, no truck, no jeep... Spread his picture in public to everyone, everywhere... offer bounty of megabucks.*"

We and the entire department searched for him everywhere, checking each and every vehicle, airplanes, trains, buses. Blocking highways, traffic signals, and took every possible step to reach Victor but in vain. He escaped but it's sure he's in the city.

We reached back to headquarters.

"*Sir, Belinda is not speaking a word*" said Addy as I reached my cabin.

"*Okay drop her home, we'll talk to her tomorrow, she's scared*" I replied him.

"*Okay*" he said and left the cabin leaving me alone. I switched on the television.

(On the Television)

"*Our ICCB's SID team led by Our Top Cop, Charles Beckett has rescued the girl unharmed today morning*" stated the commissioner, outside his office.

"*Sir what about the culprit?*" questioned one of the reporters to the commissioner.

"*Our team is on it... we'll catch him soon*" he answered and went inside ignoring any further questions.

(Phone Ringing)

Commissioner Sir Calling flashed my phone screen. I knew he would call me.

"*Hello, sir*" I wished him as soon as I received his call.

"*Hello Charles, any update about Victor*" he questioned me.

"*No sir, we are on alert, if he tries to leave the city, he would be caught*" I assured him.

"*But what if he doesn't even try and create nuisance in the city again*" he doubted. And maybe he's right, but maybe he would not.

"*Don't worry sir, we'll catch him*" I assured him again to which he replied "*Fast Charles, fast*" and we ended the call.

***

I went home, very tired. But as soon as I reached home, Chadd came running and hugged me tight. All my stress, tiredness, worries are gone just by his hug. Andrea too followed him and hugged me, by now I was completely stress-free.

"*Well done dad*" said Andrea, and listening to which I was as happy as Belinda's mother would be now after meeting her missing daughter.

"*Good job, darling*" said Amanda who was standing little far and smiling seeing us. I think they have seen Commissioner's interview on television.

"*Dad I want to be like you, dad, the top cop*" said my son, listening to this I was on seventh floor of heaven. This is what keeps me motivated towards work.

"*Sure, Chadd*" I replied him as I kissed him on his cheeks and continued "Once you grow old like me, you'll in fact be better cop than me"

"*No dad... I want to become nowww*" he replied, cutely. I couldn't reply him, so I just smiled and went inside.

"*Where are you going? You must be hungry, come dinner is ready*" said my wife. And yes, I'm actually hungry.

A lovely dinner with lovable family is what a man wants after coming back from a long day at work.

I was not able to sleep the whole night, disappointed about Victor's escapes. But now breakfast with family is what I needed the most. Andrea and Chadd having fun at the table, Amanda served us and soon joined, this is what we men live for. I wanted to go late today, stay a little longer at home. Soon Chadd left for school followed by Amanda and Andrea. I decided to watch television for a while and then leave.

I switched on the television.

(On the Television)

"I'm the actual culprit." "I ruined his life, I don't deserve to live." "One day, I was drunk, and then I saw him." "Wearing Tight White T-shirt and Blue Jeans, he was looking hot, walking alone in the mid of the night."

"I thought it's my chance now, so I did it... yes I...... him..." "Why would I stop also?" "Since my childhood my parents, teachers, elders, and everyone in the society made me realize that females are dominant to males."

"Whenever I cry, they said 'Why are you crying? Are you a boy?' so that means Boys are weaker than us."

"Whenever I worry about myself, they said 'Why are you worried? Are you a boy?' so that means Boys need to worry not us."

"Whenever my elder brother wanted to go out, they opposed to not to let him go alone, they said 'Go with a Girl' so that means they are not supposed to go alone because they are weak and we are stronger."

"Whenever my elder brother wanted to go out at night, they refused, they said 'You're not a girl to go out at this time' so that means we, girls have more rights than they."

"Whenever I lose a fight, they laughed, they said 'Why you lost? Are you a boy?' so that means boys are supposed to lose and girls win all the time."

"Whenever a boy slapped me, they laughed, they said 'How can you get beaten up by a boy?' so that means boys cannot beat girls and we're stronger & we've right to do so."

"They cannot wear tight, short clothes, we can. They cannot talk louder, we can. They cannot go out alone, we can. They cannot go out at night, we can. They cannot ride a bike, we can. They cannot drive a car, we can. They cannot earn money, we can. They cannot run a business, we can. They cannot fight with anyone, we can. They cannot defend, we can. They cannot do whatever they want, we can."

"We're strong enough to fight, not they. We've strength enough to defend, not they. They've to wash our clothes, clean our dishes, serve us; not we for them. If we do so then we're labeled as slaves, but if they do it is said to be that way."

"Doesn't that mean they're our slaves, we can dominant them? Doesn't that mean they're weaker than us, and we can use our strength on them? Doesn't that mean they can get beaten up by us, and not we? Doesn't that mean they've to do everything we say and we can order them? Doesn't that mean we can roam around anytime, anywhere wearing anything and they can't? Doesn't that mean we've independence to do our will and not they? Doesn't that mean we've dominance over them?"

"Doesn't that mean we can do whatever we want with them and they can't even defend? Doesn't that mean we've strength, we've powers, we've rights, we've independence and so we can do anything with anyone especially with them and they can't even defend or fight back?" said Belinda holding a gun at her head and shoot herself.

"This is the girl who was rescued yesterday by Top Cop Charles Beckett and SID team from an anonymous guy named Victor. She killed herself an hour ago after going live on internet from her residence" said the reporter of the news channel.

And continued "*The question here is, haven't ICCB counselled her before leaving her? Haven't they investigated the case correctly?*" pointed the news reporter. I switched off the television. They've no work other than just blaming others. I thought, I would talk to her, today, but.

I left for office and all the way, I was thinking only about Belinda and whatever she said.

She is right, the increase number of rape, assaults cases in our nation and in the entire world, proves it. Non-governmental organizations and civilians comes out on roads and protest with candles to get the culprit punished hard, I support them.

But anybody thought how to prevent it? Punishing such cheap people is a great thing to do for humanity. But do you really think giving them hard punishment would stop future crimes?

No, I'm not saying to not to punish them. But thinking that it would stop future crimes is waste. No, it won't. Then what we should do to stop such crimes from happening in future?

Remember what Belinda said? (Read it again). She gave us the answer to our question.

The Stereotypes, thinking, saying and believing that one gender has more rights, power, strength, freedom over another gender.

We should stop saying such phrases that might intentionally and eventually make one gender think that they've dominance over other. We should put some equal rights, rules for everyone regardless of their gender.

I personally have seen people, who doesn't send their son alone even if he's above 20-years-old, and send their 16-years-old daughter with him. What it might look like to her? That she is stronger than her 4-year older brother?

All these thoughts ended when I reached the office. I went straight to my cabin, responding few officers who wished me. And sat on my chair.

"*Sir*" called Addy as he came into my cabin and continued "*There's a call for you.*"

I picked up the receiver on my desk and said "*Hello.*"

"*Hey Officer*" replied a voice, on the other side of the call, I guess I'm familiar to this voice.

"*Who's this?*" I questioned as I didn't recognize his voice, though it looked familiar.

"*Victor*" he replied.

"*Victor… you can surrender… I'll help you*" I offered him.

"*Amsteria National School is my* **HOSTAGE**" he said and ended the call. There's where Amanda teaches and Andrea Studies.

...To Be Continued